To Noah, Sky, and Isla.. I am so proud to share you with the world — jg

Little ★ BOOST
is published by Picture Window Books, A Capstone Imprint
151 Good Counsel Drive, P.O. Box 669
Mankato, Minnesota 56002
www.capstonepub.com

Library of Congress Cataloging-in-Publication data is available on the Library of Congress website.
ISBN: 978-1-4048-6358-3 (library binding)

Summary: Eleanore does not like to share and soon learns a valuable life lesson about sharing and friendships.

Creative Direction: Heather Kindseth
Art Direction/Graphic Design: Kay Fraser

Eleanore

WON'T Share

by Julie Gassman   illustrated by Jessica Mikhail

PICTURE WINDOW BOOKS

a capstone imprint

ELeaNoRe was a sweet girl.
She really was.

But Eleanore had a problem.

A BIG PRObLEM.

ELEANORE did NOT
Like to shaRE.

So Eleanore made a list of rules
to make sharing easier.

1. Always share things you don't like.

2. Always share things that belong to other people.

3. Always share when it makes things more fun . . . for you!

When Eleanore got a bag of jellybeans,
she sorted them by color.

She gave the black ones away and ate the rest.

"The black ones are yucky!"
Eleanore said.

Eleanore **did Not Like SHaRiNG** her dolls.

But she always used the doll clothes her friend brought over.

"I just love sharing your things," Eleanore said.

ELeaNoRe NeveR wanted to shaRe her blocks —
unless she needed someone to play with.

"See? Aren't you having fun sharing with me?"
Eleanore said.

At school, Eleanore tried to follow the classroom rules. She didn't mind **SHARING** her snack.

"You can have my grapes," she told the boy next to her. **"I DON'T REALLY LIKE** healthy things."

She didn't mind **shaRing** at the art station, either.
It was always more fun to paint with a partner.

But Eleanore DID mind sharing at the dress-up station.

"Please **don't touch** that sparkly gown!"

"Um, **I was using** that cowboy hat."

"Excuse me, but **I Need** that vest for my outfit."

Eleanore knew she should share the clothes.
But according to her SHARING RULES,
she didn't have to.

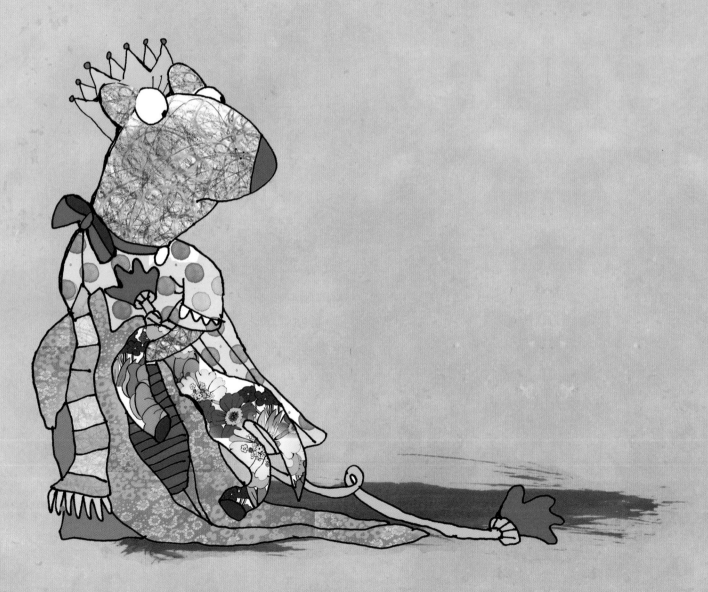

So, every day, Eleanore would take all of the
dress-up clothes for herself.

The other kids were **NOT happy** about it.

Soon, they stopped playing with the dress-up clothes — and with Eleanore.

One day, Miss Ellen taught everyone a new game.

While Eleanore was hoarding all the dress-up clothes,
the other kids were laughing, jumping, and dancing around.

Eleanore collected all the clothes and headed over to the game.

"CAN I PLAy the NeW gaMe?"

Eleanore asked. But nobody heard her.

This time everyone heard her,
but nobody seemed to care.

"It's Not faiR," Eleanore said. "You are supposed to let everyone play."

"We don't want to play with someone who doesn't share," Stevie said.

"That's Not veRy Nice,"

Eleanore said.

"Neither is hogging the dress-up clothes," Maggie said.

Eleanore thought hard.

Then she took off
the **cowboy** hat.

She took off
the **vest**, too.

And finally, she took
off the fancy gown
and **crown**.

The other kids let her play the new game.

After class, Miss Ellen whispered to Eleanore, "It's always good to share, even when you don't want to."

Eleanore whispered back, "From now on I will **tRy to shaRe** – even when **I doN't waNt to.**"

"That's great!" Miss Ellen said.

"Miss Ellen?" Eleanore asked.

"There is something I want to share with you right now."

"What's that?" asked Miss Ellen.

"A hug!"